KC Cracks the Code!

By Yvonne Lamey

Illustrated by Kezzia Crossley

KC Cracks the Code!

ISBN 13: 978-1496003133

ISBN 10: 1496003136

Acknowledgments

This is a fantasy story-a fairy tale-about KC Munchkin, a boy named Donald and the meaning of friendship and hope. The story is not hard science. But we can hope that one day, cancer and other devastating illnesses can be cured at the basic DNA level.

Many thanks to Ed Averett for inspiration, for introducing me to his amazing little KC character and creating a learning experience for me. This story and Ed's video game 'KC Returns!', hopefully, will excite young minds to find cures. Learn more about 'KC Returns!' at: kcmunchkin.com.

Gratitude to Kezzia Crossley who brought the story to life with her wonderful illustrations.

Thank you to my husband, Jack, who has had to accept a distracted wife as normal, and for the patience to wait me out.

I love you, Jacob, for your astute observations and advice on this project. And, thanks to all whose ears I have 'bent' with questions and chatter.

Yvonne Lamey

Not too long ago, there was a brave boy named

DONALD.   1

He was 6 years old when he started feeling BAD!

When he played with his friends, he got very tired.
If he fell, he'd get a BIG bruise.

His bones hurt and he had headaches too.

3

When he went inside to rest, Mom would say, "Donald, I know what will make you feel better- ice cream!" But his tummy was often queasy.

Not even ice cream sounded good.

Mom and Dad tried to do everything
right for Donald. They made sure he took his
vitamins, ate healthy food, stayed active and got
good sleep. But he was not getting better.

Mom and Dad were worried.

Donald had an imaginary friend. His name was
KC. He was a Munchkin. He was chubby-faced,
bright blue and had special magical powers.
6   He had bebops on his head too.

Donald was KC's best friend in the whole world!
They loved each other very much.

KC was always ready to listen whenever Donald
needed him. They talked about so many things-
even about how bad Donald felt.

One night at bedtime, Donald told KC that he was going to see some really smart doctors who might be able to help him feel better.

8

Dr. Smartkind was the chief doctor.

Donald and KC really liked her name! 9

The day came for Donald and his parents to meet Dr. Smartkind. They drove away and KC waited in the middle of Donald's bed on his fluffy quilt. He waited and waited and...waited.

He missed Donald a lot! But he knew that if Donald needed him, he'd call to him. After all, they were best friends!

When Donald got to the clinic where Dr. Smartkind
worked, everyone was very nice.
Donald was a bit scared.

They all did their best to help the family
feel comfortable.

Across the miles KC was listening hard for Donald,
so hard......

HE TURNED RED!!

Then he heard Donald. He was sad and very scared. Dr Smartkind tried to be gentle but the news was NOT GOOD!

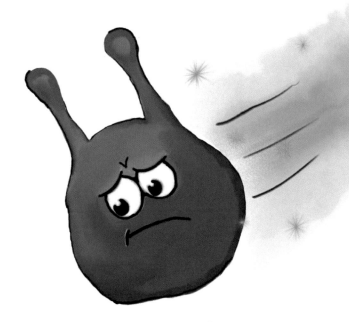

KC rushed to his friend as fast as he could!

She said, "Donald, our bodies are built of good cells-hair, bone, muscle-all kinds. But some of your cells have changed into BAD cells. More will change unless...

their broken DNA could be fixed."

Donald and his parents were puzzled. DNA?
Dad asked, "What is it?" Dr Smartkind explained,
"DNA is like the brain inside a cell.
It tells the cell what to do."

Since Donald's DNA was broken, the cells were
not behaving!   15

Donald would have to take yucky medicine to
kill the bad cells. It might make him sick
for a while. But if the medicine worked, he could
be well. This was the only thing for the doctors
to do until they learned how to fix DNA.

16

Donald didn't want to take that yucky medicine and feel sick. It would take 3 or 4 treatments for the doctors to know if it was working.

So Donald and Mom and Dad went home to get ready. He'd go back to the clinic in 1 week.

No one knew, except Donald, that KC had been at the clinic too. He listened VERY hard to learn why his best friend was sick.

He knew he must try to help!

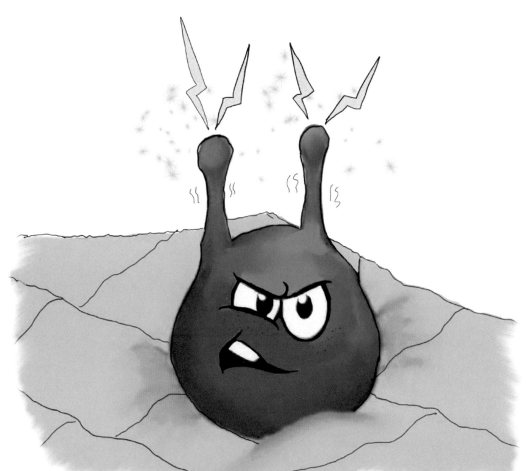

That night, in Donald's room, he and KC had a long talk. KC was angry his best friend had to go through this. He prepared for battle! KC mustered his magical strength and charged his bebops. 19

They made a plan. KC was going inside
Donald's body to find that broken DNA!

He told Donald he'd be gone for a little while—
he'd be fighting!

He asked Donald to hold out his hand.
KC jumped into his palm.
Donald saw KC's beautiful blue light.
He felt something warm and pleasant and...

POOF!!

KC WAS INSIDE!

Wow, what a wonderful place, KC thought. He got to work and went straight to Donald's heart. It was strong and good!

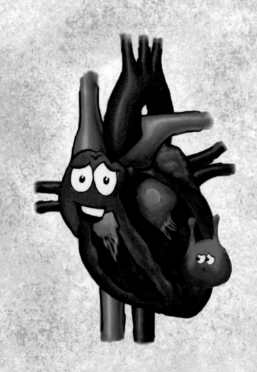

Then he SAW them...

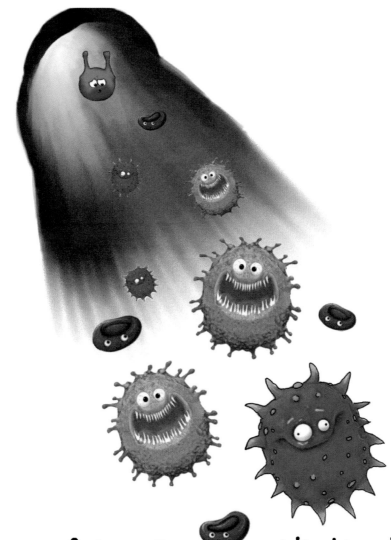

Some of the cells in Donald's blood had a
strange shape and weren't the right color.
Were these the bad ones?

KC jumped onto one of the strange cells
and went inside.

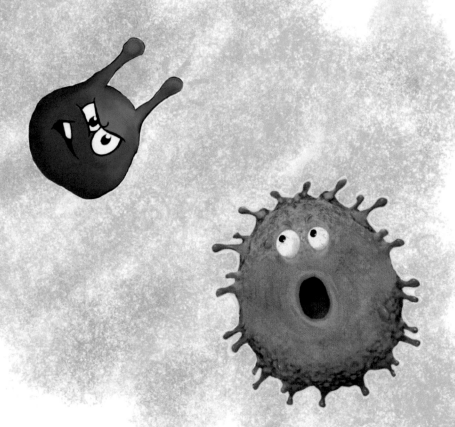

He was astounded by what he saw!

There were particles and inside of them were beautiful whirling strands. When he looked closely, he could see that some strands were torn.

This was the BROKEN DNA!

KC saw what he had to do next!

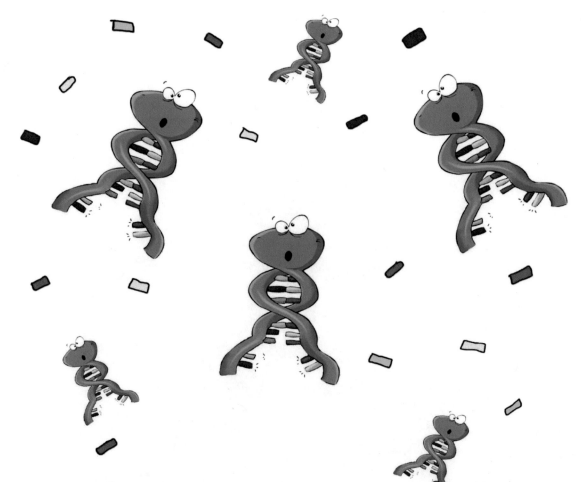

He had to put those broken strands back together.

KC grabbed a broken strand.
He held on with all his might as it whirled around!

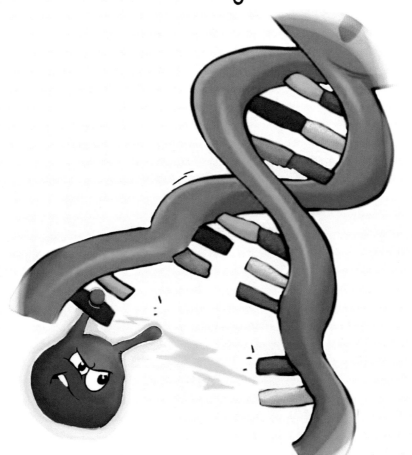

What if it broke off? It would be a very bad thing.
It would be bad for Donald!
27

His magical bebops flashed like lightning!
He took careful aim and fired his power
at the break in the strand.

There were sparks and bangs and booms!
KC couldn't see what had happened but
28   he knew what he was hoping....

When the flashes and sparks had cleared,

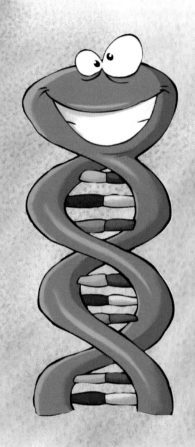

there before KC was the strand.
It was whole, beautiful, whirling and...FIXED!

29

KC went to work.
Each time he found a broken strand, he attacked!
He fought hard until they were all fixed.

But he knew he must get back to Donald.
His best friend's love kept him strong.
They depended on each other!

KC took one last look around. He was proud.
He had done a good job.

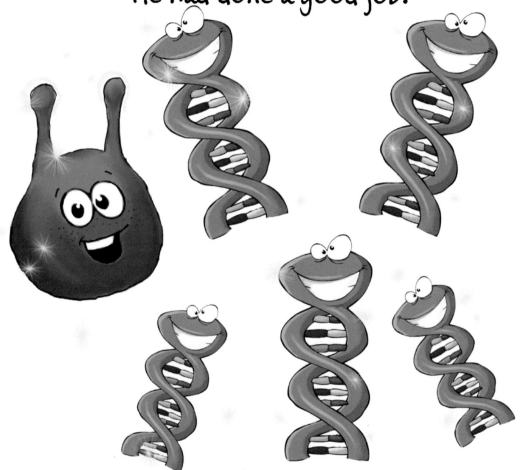

Most of all, he hoped Donald could get well now!

When Donald woke up in the morning, he knew something was different. He was glad to see the sun. He was happy to get up and eat breakfast.

32 He felt GOOD and he wanted to tell KC!

But where was KC? He'd been gone all night.
Where was he now? Was he OK?
Donald called to him.

No answer...

Donald went down and ate breakfast.
It was good but he wanted KC with him.

Donald went back to his room and called again.
Then, he noticed a warm pleasant feeling in
his palm. It was small and weak. Could it be?

Donald looked...

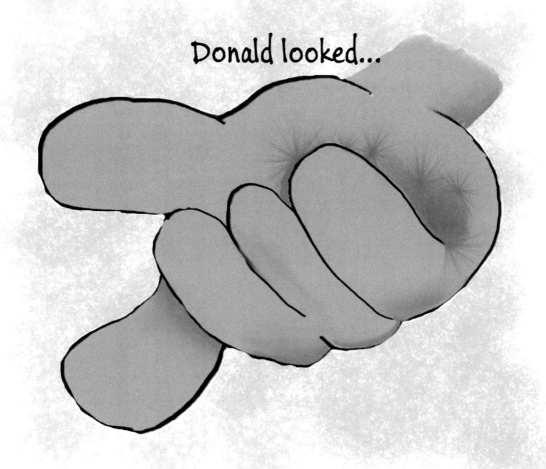

35

THERE WAS KC!

His face looked tired and his bebops were drooping.

36

Donald laughed out loud and smiled his biggest
smile. He held KC up. KC smiled back with a
weak little smile. Then, their love for
each other started to work.

KC got stronger and stronger...and happier and
happier... and bluer and bluer!

Soon they were dancing all around Donald's room. It was a celebration! They were together again and Donald was...WELL!

38

Mom and Dad heard the laughter and went to Donald's room. He told them that KC had fixed his DNA and he felt wonderful!

His parents were VERY happy but....
"Who is KC?" they asked.

Donald smiled and placed KC in their hands.
They felt something warm and pleasant and
saw a beautiful blue light.

When they saw little KC, they giggled and cheered.
KC had helped their son get well.
Then they ALL danced and danced!

The next day, KC met Dr Smartkind and he told
her what he had seen and done inside Donald's cells.
He knew that if he could see it, he could solve it.

She told KC that he was a hero!

Donald, that brave boy, became a great scientist and KC was the most famous Munchkin in the world. They helped many people get well and had a BAZILLION friends!

But despite all their fame, KC and Donald stayed BEST FRIENDS FOREVER.

THE END

Made in the USA
Las Vegas, NV
27 April 2022

48050548R00029